MONEY-GO-ROUND

Roger McGough

illustrated by

Mini Grey

WALKER BOOKS
AND SUBSIDIARIES
LONDON · BOSTON · SYDNEY · AUCKLAND

Mr Toad parked his car outside The Tree House Hotel.

"This looks pleasant," he thought, as he hopped eagerly up to the entrance. "Smart door," he said to himself.

Miss Lavender Mole, behind the reception desk, smiled a warm welcome.

"I'd like a room," said Mr Toad.

"Then you've come to the right place," replied Miss Mole. "As a matter of fact, things are very quiet at this time of the year, so you have a choice of rooms."

"In that case I'll have the biggest and the best for a week. How much will that be?"

"One gold piece," said Miss Mole.

Mr Toad banged the coin onto the counter. "I'll take it. Please put my suitcase in the room while I go for a stroll around the village. See you later this afternoon."

He hopped towards the exit. "Smartly painted door," he called, before shutting it firmly behind him.

Miss Lavender Mole held
the gleaming coin in
her paw and imagined
herself in a new hat and
scarlet coat, treating
her best friend Betty
to high tea at the Ritz.
Then she looked at the
door. "Smartly painted
indeed," she thought,
and she still hadn't paid
Sam Stoat for doing it.
Her mind made up,
Lavender slipped the
coin into her pocket and
went in search of Sam.

She didn't go far. She heard the whistling first, and there was Sam high up on a ladder, painting Widow Rabbit's windows.

"Here's the money I owe you for painting the front door of the hotel last week. Very smart it looks."

"Much obliged," said Sam. "Now I'll be able to take Samantha to see *The Wind in the Willows* at the theatre on Saturday."

He waved goodbye to Miss Mole and went back to his whistling and painting.

Then stopped. The brush he was holding reminded him of the money he owed Badger. **Badger's Bristles for the Best Brushes in the Business.** Sam couldn't fault that slogan, so he slid down the ladder and cycled off in search of Basil.

He didn't go far. Basil was busy having a nap at the back of his brush and bristle shop when Sam arrived, still whistling. "Here's the gold coin I owe you Mr Badger, many thanks." The debt paid, Sam cycled back to add a second coat of gloss paint to the widow's windows.

Wide awake now, Basil felt the warm weight of the coin in his paw. He was about to amble down to the Red Lion for a game of skittles, when he remembered he hadn't paid young Walter Water Rat for the boat trip his family had enjoyed the previous weekend.

"Better use this to pay what I owe now," he reasoned, "otherwise one game of skittles may lead to another, and another…"

Young Walter was sitting in his boat admiring his brand new jetty when Basil arrived slightly out of puff and tossed him the coin, which reflected on the surface of the river like a darting goldfish.

"What's that for?" asked the rat.

"What I owe you for taking the missus and the grandkids down to Seaport last weekend. They had a fine old time."

"Oh, I'd have done it for nothing," said Walter.

"A debt is a debt until it's repaid," replied the badger, then trundled back up the hill to scatter some skittles.

Thankful for the timely gold coin,
Walter knew exactly what he was
going to do with it: pay the otters the
rest of the money he owed them for
building his fine new jetty. He cast off,
dipped his oars into the water and
rowed steadily downriver. And as he
rowed, the sun at his back, the wind
in his whiskers, he sang an otter song.

"*A river's what an otter loves,*
And what an otter needs
Is a lotta other otters
To potter about in the reeds

To make water slides and diving pools
And dams to flood the banks,
Besotted am I with otters —
When I spot otters, I give thanks."

And spot the otters he did, on rounding a bend in the river. They were building a paddling pool for the young squirrels of the neighbourhood.

"Sorry, can't stay long," said Walter. "Just called to pay you for the jetty. Lovely job you did." He handed over the gold piece to Ozzie.

"Need a receipt?" asked Carlotta.

"No thanks," said Walter, then swung the boat around and rowed upstream.

"Such a nice young water rat," said Carlotta. "And such perfect manners."

"Perfect timing, too," said Ozzie. "Now we can pay the weasels for all the rope we bought – a debt that's been hanging over us like a heavy storm cloud these past few weeks. If we don't pay up, and quickly, they might turn nasty."

"Surely not," said Carlotta.

The weasels weren't nasty, not really. But they were good at pretending to be. When they wanted something, or a creature made them cross, they could make themselves look very fierce, and their blood-curdling screams were the result of weeks of practice.

Nervously clutching the gold coin, Carlotta took a deep breath and walked straight into their den.

"Here's the money," she said.

"What money?" said Phil, the Chief Weasel.

"The money we owe you."

"Oh yes," said the Chief Weasel, "money for old rope." And that was that.

OLD

ROPE slightly used

Phil's wife, Francesca by name, was
famous the Wild Woods over, not
only for the bushiness of her tail but
for the shininess of her claws, which she
held out for the gang to admire.

"Lovely, aren't they?"

Everybody agreed they were the
prettiest claws for miles around.

"Which reminds me," said Francesca,
"on my last visit to the Nail & Claw
salon I didn't have my purse. It was so
embarrassing. Here darling, scamper
along to the salon and
give the gold coin to Mrs
Magpie, will you."

Without a word, the
Chief Weasel did exactly
as he was told.

NAIL & CLAW

Miss Mole, wearing spectacles and a worried expression, sat at her desk doing the hotel accounts. The cash box was empty. She knew that somebody owed her money, but who?

"Cheer up Lavender," she said to herself. "Summer is on its way and soon the hotel will be filled with guests."

Just then, her one and only guest swept into the hotel.

"Ah, Mr Toad," she cried. "Have you had a pleasant afternoon?"

"Excellent, thank you. But I'm afraid I have some rather bad news. For who should I bump into in the village, but my old friends Lord and Lady Winkle."

Miss Mole removed her spectacles. "Ah, the owners of Winkle Castle, you mean?"

"Yes indeed, and they have kindly invited me to put up there for a week."

"Then you must certainly accept their offer," said Miss Mole.

"I already have done, thank you. Now while I go up to the room and fetch my suitcase, would you be kind enough to find the gold coin I gave you earlier?"

As Mr Toad hopped breezily up the stairs, Miss Mole looked again into the empty cash box. Her heart pounded as the awful truth dawned: not only could she not return the gold coin to Mr Toad, but now she was actually in debt!

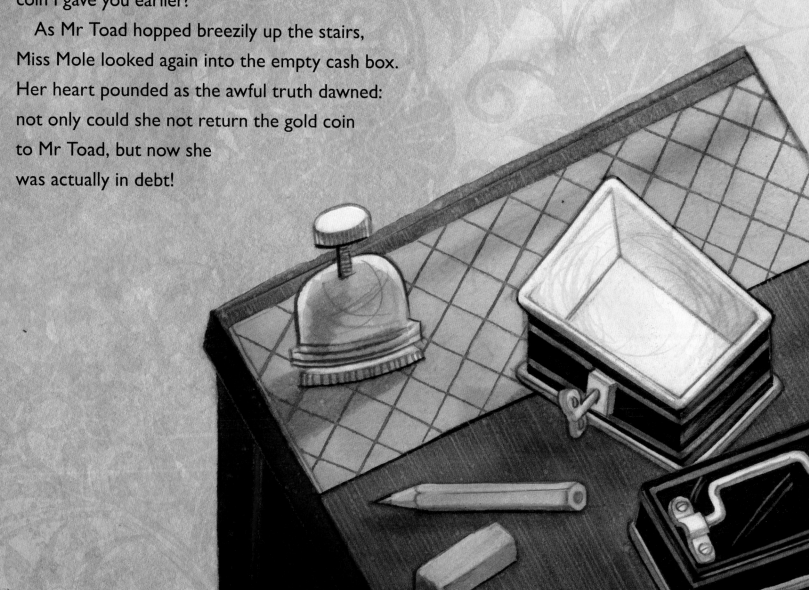

Suddenly, there was a rush of air followed by a flapping sound as a young magpie flew excitedly around the room and landed on the desk. In its beak was a bright gold coin, which it dropped before Miss Mole.

"Mother said thank you for letting us hire the room for Grandma's birthday party, and sorry for being late paying our bill."

Miss Mole looked on in amazement as the magpie rose into the air and flew towards the open window, where she hovered.

"Oh, I nearly forgot. Mother said the next time you are passing the Nail & Claw salon, please drop in for a free polish." With that she disappeared.

Lavender Mole clasped the coin in both paws, her face aglow.

"What perfect timing," she cried.

"Perfect!" said Mr Toad, who bounded into the hall and pocketed the coin.

THE END

... well, almost.

THE WILD WOOD BUGLE

Local News For Local Animals

TOAD FOUND GUILTY

Mr Donald Toad, of no fixed address, pleaded guilty in court today to forging a gold coin. The naughty creature admitted he made it "for a joke" out of two jam jar lids glued together and painted gold. Mr Justice Bull said that in Mr Toad's defence, the coin had not been used to purchase goods, having been in Miss Lavender Mole's safekeeping all afternoon. The accused was let off with a stern warning and promised never to be naughty again.

SQUIRREL POOL

A paddling pool for baby and toddler squirrels was opened yesterday, thanks to the efforts of Ozzie and Carlotta Otter and their family. Safe and sound, youngsters both red and grey can splash around every day. Admission free.

Book Festival

The literary festival held last week in the village school was a huge success. Peter Rabbit talked about his life with Beatrix Potter, and Francesca Weasel received warm paws-applause after reading from her new book about fairies. Poems fluttered from the Poetree on the lawn and there was cherry cake.

THEATRE REVIEW

"The Wind in the Willows on Ice"
A new musical with lots of slides

The Wild Wood Theatre was transformed into a winter wonderland for this spectacular show, which opened last night. Breathtaking! The skates hissed, but the crowd cheered.

"BRUSHES I HAVE KNOWN" A NEW EXHIBITION BY SAM STOAT

Art Exhibition

Local artist Sam Stoat will display his work at Winkle Castle in November. A popular painter and decorator, Sam hopes that the exhibition will enable him to fulfil his dream of becoming a full-time artist.

POETRY CORNER

GRANDMA DAY

Elderflowers are the perfect flowers
To give gran on Grandma Day,
For though she may be elderly
She loves a sweet bouquet.

Francesca Weasel

MOTORFEST

Next Saturday at Winkle Castle

- Free rides in noisy, fast cars
- For petrol-heads of all shapes and sizes
- Kids' fancy dress
- Clowns in dodgems
- All the fun of the garage

(All proceeds go to "Save the Bees")

THE TREE HOUSE HOTEL

A warm welcome awaits.
Comfy beds and good food.

BADGER'S BRISTLES

For the best brushes in the business

LOCAL DENTIST

Tooth a bit squiffy?
I'll have it out in a jiffy.
(Price: 2 nuts per molar)
Sadiq Squirrel BDM

Lonely Hearts

Fe-mole seeks he-mole for friendship. Write c/o The Tree House Hotel

NAIL & CLAW SALON

Grooming & preening. Claws buffed, feathers re-fluffed. Fleas and ticks removed in strict confidence.
PAYMENT: anything shiny

LENGI'S CAFÉ

Fresh fish, locally caught, featuring …

fish fingers, fish fritters, fish cakes, fish n fish, fish crumble and custard. Cooked by our own chef, Otter Lengi.

www.com

The Wild Wood Web company is now up and spinning! All our webs are spun to perfection by local spiders, and are ideal for use as hair nets or fishing nets, or simply for decorating that dark room in the house that everybody is too scared to go into.

WINKLE-PICKERS

Strawberry pickers wanted for seasonal work on the fruit farm at Winkle Castle. Good rates.

WEASEL'S OLD ROPE

For all your old rope needs.
Reef knot, Granny knot,
Perhaps knot, Afraid knot,
Simply knot, Why knot?

QUICK SALE

One Toadster racing car.
Brand new (almost).
Hardly used (during the night).
Owner turning over new leaf.
Cash only, no questions asked.

FANCY A GAME OF SKITTLES?

Then scuttle along to the Red Lion and scatter a few. Sharpen your skittle skills and make new friends.

THE ACORN CINEMA

Frankly, my deer…

NOW SHOWING…

Gone with the Wind, Nuts in May, Tales from the Riverbank, Star Paws, Harry Otter and the Giblet of Fire

RIVER TRIPS

Upstream
Downstream
We all scream
For Walter Rat

Find him at his new jetty.

Come for a tootle
In his new boat "The Bootle"

Tree House Hotel Wins Award.

Miss Lavender Mole was delighted to receive the Wild Wood's most coveted award at a ceremony at Winkle Castle last week. Said Lady Winkle, who presented the recyclable silver cup, "Congratulations!"

Acrossword

1 What weasels sell (3,4)
2 Lord and Lady _ _ _ _ _ _ (6)
3 Basil's favourite game (8)
4 3 x 7 – 2 (2)
5 Miss Mole's best friend (5)
6 Nail & _ _ _ _ Salon (4)
7 What the otters built for Walter (5)
8 The finish (3,3)

ANSWERS: (1) Old rope, (2) Winkle, (3) Skittles, (4) 19, (5) Betty, (6) Claw, (7) Jetty, (8) The End

STOP PRESS!
(Saved from the nick in the nick of time!)
Mr Toad was saved from bankruptcy yesterday when his friends Lord and Lady Winkle paid off all his debts. "We hope he has learned his lesson," they said. "And by living within his means and not overspending he can live happily ever after."

For Bobby, Lola and Silvan – RM^cG • *To Auntie Rita and Cousin Tone* – MG

First published 2020 by Walker Books Ltd, 87 Vauxhall Walk, London SE11 5HJ • 10 9 8 7 6 5 4 3 2 1 • Text © 2019 Roger McGough • Illustrations © 2019 Mini Grey • The right of Roger McGough and Mini Grey to be identified as author and illustrator respectively of this work has been asserted by them in accordance with the Copyright, Designs and Patents Act 1988 • This book has been typeset in Gill Sans • Printed in China • All rights reserved. No part of this book may be reproduced, transmitted or stored in an information retrieval system in any form or by any means, graphic, electronic or mechanical, including photocopying, taping and recording, without prior written permission from the publisher. • British Library Cataloguing in Publication Data: a catalogue record for this book is available from the British Library • ISBN 978-1-4063-8135-1 • www.walker.co.uk